AF426466

Forgiving Jake

Scott De Buitléir

MKB Publishing, 2020

Copyright © 2020 Scott De Buitléir

All rights reserved. This book or any portion thereof may not be reproduced or used in any manner whatsoever without the express written permission of the publisher, except for the use of brief quotations in a book review.

First Printing, 2020

ISBN 9780463472101 (ebook)
ISBN 9798635310687 (Print)

Published by MKB Publishing
Dublin, Ireland

www.scottdebuitleir.com

Scott De Buitléir is an author and poet from Dublin, Ireland. He lives in Cork city in the southwest of Ireland with his partner, and loves to travel. While he has published works of poetry and non-fiction before, this is his first novella. You can follow him on Twitter at @scottdebuitleir.

Forgiving Jake

Chapters

1   17

2   28

3   37

4   46

5   52

6   59

7   70

8   76

9   85

10   92

11   99

12   108

13   116

14   126

15   137

16   146

17   152

18   162

Epilogue   173

This is a work of fiction. Names, characters, businesses, places, events, locales, and incidents are either the products of the author's imagination or used in a fictitious manner. Any resemblance to actual persons, living or dead, or actual events, is purely coincidental.

1

"This is getting ridiculous," Sarah blurted out, looking at her phone for the seventh time that minute. She didn't bother keeping her voice low. She was talking only to herself, but she didn't care who was within earshot. Her patience ran out ages ago.

It wasn't like Jake to keep her waiting on date night, although he had messaged her that morning to say that he needed to buy his mother's birthday present, after the gym and before their cinema date, so he might be a bit late. Forty minutes were not just "a bit", though. He had already bought the tickets, so she couldn't even see the movie if she wanted to. Instead, she was left to wait in the foyer, apart from the odd time she would go back onto the street to look for him.

She checked her phone yet again, searching for any trace of online activity. WhatsApp, Messenger, Snapchat, Instagram; all of them showed a *last seen* status of over three hours ago. She messaged him on almost every app, but none of them got through to his phone. Her calls just went to voicemail. Annoyingly, Jake was never too bothered to keep his phone charged, so a dead phone in the afternoon wasn't totally unheard of.

For a moment, her reflection in the glass doorway of the cinema caught her attention. A brunette in a pink hoodie and fitted jeans stood before her in the glass, wearing a little light foundation and her favourite lipstick. The reflection didn't emit the perfume Jake bought her for Christmas, but she always wore it for their date night. Thanks to Jake's new job as a security guard, that Sunday evening was the only opportunity the two had to spend some quality time together, but she still looked forward to it. Maybe a hoodie wouldn't normally be considered date night attire, she thought, but after a year of dating, their efforts were allowed to be a bit more casual, weren't they?

More people passed her in the foyer, as she tried to calm her impatience and appear nonchalant in her solitude. She scanned the faces of those who were also on a date, as if she were channelling Jake on his night duties. A muscular guy with a leather jacket and tight haircut threw his arm over the girl beside him, who blushed as she looked up at him. Two guys shared the rewards of their raid at the snack counter, as they made their way to where the latest superhero movie was showing. Another couple looked less happy to be together, as a blonde girl threw cold looks at her date, who devoured a hot dog while trying to ignore his partner. Each of them had their own story, she thought, but at least they were together.

Looking at her phone one last time, desperately wishing to see an *online* status appear beside his name, Sarah gave up and walked across the street to the café. She ordered a lattè and sat down at the window, where she could still see who was approaching the cinema, like her boyfriend, for example, and hopefully soon. Maybe once Jake saw her, he'd run to pick her up in a passionate kiss. Or, maybe before she'd run to him and punch him in the balls. Whichever felt better in the moment, she reckoned.

Another few minutes passed. Could it be that she was an hour early instead? She checked the cinema's timetable on her phone, and it proved Sarah was right. Jake was late... unless he meant the Revue Cinema instead of the Royal? It wasn't too far away, but he usually preferred the Royal, and didn't think much of the Revue. Another search showed that the Revue's next showing of Danger in Paris was in fifteen minutes, but it seemed too unlikely that Jake would mess up their plans that much.

Her phone lit up, and its ringtone battled against the grinding of the coffee machine. Sarah's heart jumped, but it was only her mother, Alice. She answered it with a frustrated, tired "Hello".

"Hey honey, what's wrong?"

"Nothing much, apart from being stood up, by the looks of it. I can't get through to Jake and he was supposed to meet me an hour ago."

"Really? That's not like him", Alice replied softly. "There's probably a good reason though. I waited for your father for three hours at a train station, once. He almost ruined our vacation!"

"How did he make up for it?"

"Well, he ended up producing a certain diamond ring at the station, so I kind of had to forgive him. He had left it at your uncle's apartment for safe keeping, but Tim lost his keys to collect it, and Uncle Frank was away in Germany!"

Sarah smiled for the first time in a while, relieving the tension in her chest a little. "I guess that was a decent excuse. I don't expect Jake to have the same one, though it still better be a good one".

"Once he doesn't produce a ring just yet, honey," her mother warned. "I like him, but it's a little early for that!"

"Mom, if he doesn't show up soon, he'll need to find another girl to ask".

"Well, maybe give him another few minutes, but come back home if you want to. I have dinner in the oven, your favourite".

Sarah thanked her mother for the advice and said goodbye, wanting to have another look at her social apps. Jake still wasn't online, but Sarah was a little calmer after the call. She imagined him running up the street with balloons, or an oversized teddy, or even a small jewellery box, all to beg forgiveness. She imagined him out of breath, with that smile he'd have whenever he knew he did something wrong. Not that he did it often, but he was still a guy. Men aren't infallible, and Jake—despite being one of the sweetest guys Sarah ever met—was just as prone to moments of idiocy as anyone else.

She opened Instagram, and noticed a new photo from her best friend, Chrissy. She had just returned from a couple of weeks in

Australia, and her profile had been full of incredible images; surfing, kangaroos, and the occasional drunken night out. Her adventures always seemed incredible, Sarah thought, but she knew that's what social media does. Add a filter to anything, and life doesn't look as lonely. Chrissy's photo was a selfie, looking out her bedroom window. The caption underneath read: "Wondering what will happen next. #newbeginnings"

Sarah decided to kill a few more minutes by calling her.

"Oh, Sarah, hey."

"So, tell me all about your 'new beginnings'," she said with a half-smile, allowing herself the distraction. "Sounds intriguing."

The other end of the phone fell silent for a second, before Sarah could hear her friend sighing.

"Look, I'm sorry. We knew he'd have to tell you eventually. You have every right to hate me."

Sarah's smile fell from her face as her concentration became fully focused on the phone call.

"Tell me eventually?"

"He said he was waiting for the right time to tell you about us. I guess he just waited until I came back home. I'm so sorry."

Sarah froze at her supposed friend's accidental confession. She could feel a twitch in her left hand as she held her phone to her ear, but that was the extent of her physical reaction to her man-stealing friend.

"Well, I'm sorry to disappoint you," Sarah replied coldly after taking a deep breath, "but your brand new boyfriend didn't break up with me to run off with you. Instead, he didn't show up at all. I don't know about you, but if a guy doesn't even have the guts to dump a girl, he's probably no good as a boyfriend. Either way, you can have him."

She put down the phone, and only then did the rage pour into her veins. Her fury was not a reaction to Jake—that would come later—but that the 'other girl' was Chrissy. She never seemed to like Jake when the three of them hung out, but it appeared her so-called best friend's tactics hid her true feelings well enough. Being betrayed by a guy is one thing, but your best friend too? That hurt more than Jake.

She knocked back the last of her lattè like a shot of tequila, and stormed out of the café.

As she quickly made her way towards her tram stop, her phone rang again. The screen displayed Margaret Roberts - Jake's mother. Sarah's rage became focused as she answered the call.

"Jake, I swear to God, if you're still in your mother's house -"

Her rant was interrupted by the sound of wailing. It didn't take her long to realise it wasn't Jake on the other end of the call.

2

"Mrs. Roberts? Maggie, what's wrong, are you alright?!"

The sobbing continued for a moment before she heard his mother attempt to speak.

"Sarah... they couldn't... they said they couldn't..."

"Maggie, where are you? What happened?"

"They couldn't save him, Sarah. He was running after Rex .... but they couldn't save him."

Sarah's heart was racing now, but not because of Chrissy.

"He's gone, Sarah. Jake's gone."

Sarah didn't even want to register what Maggie just said, so she chose to ignore it.

"Where are you?"

"C-city Hospital," Maggie's answer was forced through her sobbing. The mention of a hospital hit Sarah even harder than Maggie's previous statement.

"I'm coming over now, I'll be there in ten minutes or so. Hold on, I'm coming."

"Okay, love," Maggie replied, her voice softer.

Sarah hung up the phone, and inhaled slowly to calm her racing heart. It didn't feel like her world had stopped when she heard Maggie on the phone. People still moved around her. Cars passed by. She could hear a young girl laughing in the background.

It was only Sarah who stood still in the world, as if time and space were tearing her body out of reality. Now, the effort to pull herself back into the moment was enormous, but she knew she couldn't become a living statue. Even if she felt empty enough to be one.

The taxi sped through streets, around cars and crowds, until the hospital came into view. Once it stopped and the fare paid, Sarah ran towards the doors of the Emergency department, not knowing where else to go.

Patients and visitors stood outside, some of them ironically smoking in front of the large 'No Smoking' symbols, but one young girl stood alone. Her blonde hair was tied back in a ponytail, her pained face clear to make out. Sarah ran straight towards Jake's little sister.

"Sarah!" Mandy ran to meet her as soon as she noticed her. The two slammed into each other on the road beside a stationary ambulance, as their arms locked into a tight embrace. Sarah expected Mandy to cry upon impact, but instead, it was Sarah who fought to hold back the tears. She couldn't yet, though, she felt. It still wasn't real to her, as if she was taking part in some live-action television show. She felt like an actress, and that someone would eventually yell 'cut', so she could relax.

"Where's Jake?"

"They were operating on him, but..." Mandy's words trailed off, not knowing how to finish what she couldn't yet say.

"Mom and Dad are in the family room. I said I'd wait for you here."

"Thanks, chica," Sarah replied tenderly, as she hugged Mandy tighter for a moment, before releasing from their embrace. She took Mandy's hand in her own, and let Jake's little sister lead her into City Hospital.

The way to the Family Room felt like a maze. Left at the reception, towards the elevators, past the café and shop, where a display of greeting cards stood outside. From Happy Birthday to Get Well Soon, the cards now seemed to stir a kind of jealousy within Sarah.

Jake visited her in City Hospital the year before, when she ended up celebrating her birthday with a broken leg after a mountain biking accident. He brought her a card, one of Mandy's favourite stuffed animals, and a fashion magazine. All Sarah wanted now was to be taken back to that time, when she was the one lying in a hospital bed, not him.

***

The Sun began to set, casting an orange pink hue over the sky. Summer had been kind so far that year, but Sarah hadn't expected such a cold night.

She stood outside the hospital on her own, while Jake's family consoled each other indoors. She felt uneasy being with them for too long, but they appeared to have no idea why. They knew her as Jake's girlfriend, when in reality, she had only become his ex-girlfriend that morning.

She took out her phone and looked through her recent calls, before placing it against her ear, waiting to hear a response.

"Sarah, I don't want to fight."

"That's not why I'm calling, Chrissy." Sarah took a deep breath.

"What I'm about to say isn't some sick joke or an attempt to prank you. I'm really sorry, but I thought you needed to know, especially if you two had something."

A tense silence fell.

"Sarah, you're freaking me out. What's going on?"

"It's Jake..." Sarah's throat tightened as her eyes welled up.

"Chrissy, he's dead. He was knocked down outside his house earlier today. His family brought him to City Hospital, and the doctors tried to save him, but he didn't make it."

Chrissy didn't speak, but Sarah couldn't wait. She didn't want to break down completely while speaking to the woman who stole her boyfriend from her, the woman who destroyed Sarah's own ability to grieve properly, how a girlfriend would be expected to.

"I... I have to go here, I'm at the hospital with his family. I just thought you deserved to know sooner rather than later. I'm sorry. Bye."

She ended the call, without giving her former best friend a chance to reply. Sarah couldn't be there for her as a friend anymore, not after her betrayal, but she still felt she had to tell her the news. Maybe it was because she always told Chrissy everything, even when they were kids. Maybe it was that she needed to show off that it was she who was at the hospital, grieving with Jake's family, and not Chrissy.

Maybe she just wanted to tell her that nobody could have him, now. Or maybe it was just because she needed to tell someone, so it didn't feel as surreal.

She called her mother, asking her to pick her up from the hospital. She went back into the Family Room, where Jake's parents and little sister held each other on the sofa in the small, white space. She explained that her mother was on her way, and that she'd visit them before the funeral, not knowing if she'd be able to keep such a promise yet. She hugged them all, one by one, and said goodbye.

Passing the hospital's shop one more time, she noticed a different greeting card. It was blue, with a teddy bear in the middle and We'll Miss You in big, blue letters. She walked faster towards the exit and drop-off area outside, where she spotted her mother's car. She ran over to it, opened the door, jumped in, and aimed her head for her mother's shoulder.

Once her skin felt her mother's warmth, she cried, and cried, and cried.

3

Sunlight broke through the heavy curtains of Sarah's bedroom, illuminating the space just enough to lull her softly out of her slumber. Remembering the events of the day before, she wished she could just go back to sleep, and find solace in her dreams.

She usually made fun of herself for having a terrible memory, but she could remember everything so distinctly about the day Jake died. Waking up to a new day, remembering it all, made her start to accept her new reality, like the feeling of goosebumps spreading across skin.

Every so often, her phone would vibrate on her bedside table. Normally, she'd pick it up at a moment's notice, but it no longer seemed as important to her life.

Then, she thought of Chrissy. That was enough to prompt her to move, as she reached over to the phone. The home screen showed plenty of new messages, but she decided to send one of her own before reading anything else.

"We need to talk. In person. Meet me at Dixie's Coffeehouse at lunchtime."

Sarah dragged herself out of bed and into the shower. A fresh outfit—a black top and jeans seemed modern, yet still appropriate—and she walked downstairs to the kitchen, where her mother prepared breakfast.

Alice was how Sarah imagined she'd look at her mother's age. She possessed her family's famous cheekbones, with auburn hair, greying slighting at the sides, and always dressed with a sophisticated flair.

Sarah knew Alice had been up for a few hours, but wouldn't disturb her daughter until she was ready to emerge. Alice knew everything that Sarah needed, from space to her favourite food, and Sarah loved her mother for the strength of that unspoken bond.

"Good morning, love", Alice greeted, once she heard Sarah's footsteps on the kitchen's tiles.

"I'm making crêpes, any special requests?"

"Nutella, please".

Alice wouldn't normally allow a 'dessert' topping, but these were exceptional times. She reached for the spread jar from a cabinet nearby, and decorated the crêpes to her daughter's liking.

"Any plans for today", her mother asked cautiously, "or will you just take it easy here?"

"No, I've already made plans to see Chrissy down at Dixie's."

"Oh, that'll be nice," Alice replied, sounding relieved. "She's always there for you."

"Yeah, except when she was hoping to steal my man."

"What?!"

"Jake was apparently going to break up with me yesterday. Chrissy told me on the phone that they had been seeing each other before she went to Australia. Three months ago."

"Oh, Sarah... I don't know what to say."

Sarah allowed herself to regard her mother's last utterance as being rhetorical, as she poured a cup of freshly-made coffee from their cafetière. She looked back up at Alice after a moment, noticing that her facial expression had become much more concerned than before.

"Don't worry, Mom. I'm not going to be getting into a cat fight."

Dixie's Coffeehouse must have been the original inspiration for half of the Starbucks décor in Toronto, Sarah thought to herself, as she entered the café that had been part of her life for so long. She had worked there when it opened its doors to the city's students, hipsters, morning-rush businesspeople, yummie mummies, and Jake.

She spilled an entire iced coffee onto his lap when she first met him, and it took him a further two years to pluck up the courage to ask her out on a date. Dixie's was like a second home to Sarah, yet she wasn't sure whether or not Jake's death had now tainted the place.

After ordering a cappuccino from the ever-friendly Tim, she sat down in a quiet corner of the coffeehouse, where she waited on Chrissy to arrive. When she did, there was no warm "Hi", no getting up from her seat to hug her, no "Oh my god, it's been so long". She just looked at Chrissy as she cautiously approached the table.

"Hey."

"So, I have two things to say," Sarah began. "The first is that I'm not going to scream at you, I'm not going to hit you, and I'm not going to be a drama queen about this. But if everything you said yesterday was true, then you've spent a long time betraying me, and I need to know a few things."

Chrissy looked away as she pulled her blonde hair behind her left ear.

"Sarah, I'm so sorry -"

"No," Sarah interrupted firmly, trying not to shout. "No 'sorry'. No condolences. Tell me everything."

Taking a slow, deep breath, Chrissy told Sarah the whole story. How Jake was there for her when her dad was diagnosed with cancer last Christmas. How they'd occasionally text each other at first, but then it got a little more frequent. Then, on a Friday night out, a stolen kiss on the street.

Sarah listened intently to every detail, making sure not to show any reaction to Chrissy's story. Every word cut her deeply, but she wouldn't dare show her pain to the woman who stole her boyfriend.

"So, during all this, it never occurred to you to stop yourself, and say: 'Hold on a second, Jake is Sarah's boyfriend, I can't'".

"It never felt like I did anything wrong until the kiss, and then everything changed. I wanted to be with him, and saw only him. I felt like -"

"Like you were the only girl he was looking at. Yeah, he was good at giving that look, it seems."

Sarah knocked back the last of her coffee, picked her phone off the table, and put it back into her handbag.

"Alright, Chrissy. Here's how it's going to go. I'll see you at the funeral, and I'll be with his family there, because for better or worse, they didn't know anything about you, or how he felt about you. If it's any consolation, that may be painful for the two of us, because now I don't know how to be with them. So, see you at the funeral. After that, I never want to see you again. Not now, not in a few months, never. For a guy to fall for another girl is one thing, but for my friend of ten years to just forget me like that? We're done here, in more ways than one."

"Sarah, please." Chrissy's eyes started to well up, making her break eye contact with Sarah.

"I'm sorry for your loss, Christina. Goodbye."

4

Nothing could have prepared Sarah for Jake's funeral. She spent hours preparing herself for the Catholic mass at Saint Patrick's Church, but as Alice parked the car nearby, it all began to feel in vain.

Her heart started to beat strongly within her chest, as if it knew what was going to happen next, like a dog being brought to the vet. Alice noticed her daughter beginning to react to the reality of attending Jake's funeral, and grabbed her hand softly.

"Breathe. It's not going to be easy, but I'm here for you. I love you."

One slow, deep breath, and Sarah nodded, signalling to her mother that she was as ready as she could ever be. They stepped out of the car, and made their way towards the church's entrance, where Jake's family, friends, and other people gathered. Sarah quickly noticed Maggie and Mandy standing by Jake's father, Jason, and knew she had to go over to them.

None of Jake's family seemed to know anything about Chrissy, or if they did, they didn't let anything slip. Instead, they all acted and spoke to Sarah as if Jake was madly in love with her. Just like she once thought.

"Sarah, I'm so sorry," Sarah heard from behind her, while she was chit-chatting with Jake's family. She turned around to see Chrissy. Sarah was stunned. She knew she'd see her, but after their conversation at the coffeehouse, she didn't expect her to approach Sarah, let alone talk to her.

Chrissy was visibly shaken, and looked nervous, somehow. Under normal circumstances, Sarah would've given her best friend a hug and asked her if she was alright, but nothing was normal lately.

"Thank you," Sarah replied reservedly. Instead of asking how Chrissy was, Sarah instead introduced Maggie to her, so that the small talk would be diverted.

Chrissy's eyes widened when Sarah uttered the words: "Jake's mother, Maggie," but she immediately extended her hand to shake Maggie's, and told her how sorry she was for her loss. Sarah's stomach turned at that, but she knew that now was not the right time for a cat-fight, nor was it her style. Besides, this was Jake's day, regardless of how he was going to break her heart.

Soon, the crowd began to enter the church, as the coffin was taken from the hearse and the procession began, following it towards the altar. Maggie grabbed Sarah's hand without saying a word, while Mandy took her mother's hand on the other side.

Sarah looked to Alice, who nodded in acknowledgment that, whether Sarah liked it or not, she had to play the role of the heartbroken girlfriend, and therefore, part of Jake's family. She sat down at the foremost pew in the church, and Maggie invited Alice to sit next to them.

The funeral was surreal and slow, like every second carried its weight in sorrow. Sarah held her mother's hand with one hand, and Maggie's with her other hand, all throughout the mass. Later, as his coffin was lowered into the freshly-dug grave, she allowed herself to pause the pain she felt from his betrayal. Instead, just for those few moments, she cried for the young man she loved. She cried for not saying she loved him more, even despite what Chrissy had told her. She cried for the Jake she once had.

Soon, the priest finished his final prayers at the burial, and people were beginning to leave the graveyard. Sarah told Maggie and Jason that she and Alice would see them later that afternoon for the get-together at their house, and made their way back to Alice's car. As Sarah opened the passenger door to get in, she looked over at the grave and paused.

"You okay, hon?" her mother asked.

"Chrissy. She's left on her own."

Alice, unusually, didn't know what to say to her daughter's observation. There was a time when the two girls were so close, but everything was different now. Before Alice could say anything, Sarah shook her head quickly, like she had gotten the shivers, and got into the car. Alice glanced over, noticing a girl standing by the new grave, holding herself and crying.

What a mess this whole thing is, she thought to herself.

5

Weeks slowly passed after the funeral. Sarah's otherwise mediocre office job killed time quickly, but her free time in the evenings and weekends was the most painful.

She didn't reply to any of her friends' messages, and ignored any call that wasn't from her mother. She ate dinner with Alice, and mostly listened to her mother talk, because Sarah didn't really have anything to say. One night, however, Alice prepared Sarah's dinner as normal, but also presented a red envelope with it.

"What's this?"

"A little gift to cheer you up," Alice replied nonchalantly, as she sat down to her own meal.

Sarah, more curious than hungry, opened the envelope before picking up the cutlery. Inside, there was a plane ticket, with her name on it, for a flight from Toronto Pearson airport to Dublin.

"You're sending me to Ireland?"

"I think it's time for you to give yourself some time to heal and move on from everything that has happened lately," Alice replied warmly.

"The past few weeks have been difficult, and I'm not saying you need to get over it, but staying in and sinking into some reclusive state here won't help. I've arranged for your Aunt Kate to look after you for a few weeks at her place in Dublin."

Sarah didn't know what to say, but looked at the ticket again. She was set to leave in just three days. She got up from the dinner table, walked over to Alice, and gave her the warmest cuddle, just like she would as a kid.

"I love you, Mom, thank you."

Three days later, Sarah hugged her mother tightly at the airport, before going through the security check and towards her gate.

The flight across the Atlantic to Dublin took seven hours, but thankfully, Sarah slept through most of it. When she woke up, morning had broken over the undulating hills and fields of the Irish countryside underneath her, and the airplane was beginning its descent.

Dublin Airport was surprisingly modern and impressive, Sarah thought, but then again, she didn't know what to expect. The last time she was in Europe was when she was ten years old, for a family vacation to Disneyland Paris. Dad was still alive, then.

Once she got through Passport Control and collected her travel cases, Sarah walked through the Arrivals gates. Crowds had gathered on the other side, to welcome tourists and homecomers alike. One of the welcomers was her Aunt Kate, who, to Sarah, simply looked like a younger version of her mother.

"Long time no see, kiddo", Kate said softly. Her brown hair tickled Sarah's nose while she hugged her warmly, just like when she was a kid.

"Good to see you, Kate."

"Lemme take those bags. Kieran is waiting for us in the car."

Sarah walked out of the large airport terminal and to the parking lot, where her Irish uncle was waiting for them both. After hugs and initial pleasantries, Kieran drove them into Dublin City.

Dublin seemed to be a strange but fascinating place to Sarah; cute and quaint in some parts, spacious and modern in others.

As the car drove through the city and towards the suburban coastline, Kieran pointed to the large ferry sailing away from Dublin Bay, making its way to some port in Britain. There was a pace of life here that seemed calmer than Toronto, Sarah thought. Maybe that was just what she needed.

Soon, they made it to Kate and Kieran's house, complete with a golden retriever and a view of the bay. Kieran took the luggage from the car, and let Sarah soak in the surroundings of her holiday home.

"Fáilte romhat," Kieran said, much to Sarah's confusion.

"Excuse me?"

"It means you're welcome in Irish," Kieran said warmly, holding back a laugh.

"I'll teach you how to say 'Cheers!' in Irish later on, when we go down to the pub tonight!"

"Sounds good."

Kate showed Sarah to her room for the few weeks that Sarah would stay in Dublin, and she gasped at it. The room was perfect for her; brightly-lit with a balcony view of the bay, looking across to a headland in the distance. It looked like some 'Interiors' photo she'd expect to come across on Pinterest. The good weather probably helped, as Kieran mentioned she was lucky to see blue skies in Ireland at that time of the year, but it still took her breath away.

"Kate?"

"Yes hon?"

"Remind me to get Mom the biggest thank you card for this, and I'm also taking you guys out for dinner to say thanks."

Kate smiled warmly, and looked at Sarah for a moment.

"What? Is something wrong?"

"Nothing at all, Sarah. It's just good to see you. Okay, get settled in, and then I'll make some dinner here. You can take us out another evening!"

6

Sarah knew that the part of Dublin her aunt and uncle lived in was called Dalkey, and it appeared to be an idyllic village, south of the Irish capital's bustling streets.

Kieran suggested that they took things easy while Sarah got over the jet-lag, so, after a bit of food and a nap in her room, the three wandered into the village to enjoy the evening with a drink in the local pub.

It had been over fifteen years since Sarah spent any proper quality time with Kate and Kieran, when they were visiting family in Canada for a few weeks. They all reminisced about that trip, although Sarah was a little hazy on some of the visit's details, on account of her only being around five years old at the time.

She briefly caught up with them during her father's funeral, but unsurprisingly, that was something of a haze in her mind as well.

As Kieran got up from their table to go to the bar, Kate looked Sarah straight in the eye.

"So, how are you feeling?"

"Fine, I guess," Sarah replied nonchalantly. "I mean, the jet-lag isn't as bad as -"

"Sarah."

Her aunt had the exact same method of stopping someone in their tracks as her mother, calling them out if their avoidance senses were triggered. Sarah couldn't avoid her mother's finely-tuned skills, and Kate was no different, so instead, Sarah took a breath and paused before answering properly.

"I dunno. I feel hollow. I know I'm young, but I thought Jake and I were pretty solid. We had ups and downs like any couple, but he was a good guy... or so I thought. I can't really mourn for him, because in a weird way, I feel like I didn't know him in the end. If it weren't for Chrissy, I'd feel like I could miss him, but I just can't. It's like my mind is searching for an Option B, but instead, I'm getting that stupid 'buffering' thing, like on a YouTube video."

Kate grinned a little. "That's one way of putting it, I guess. Did you try talking with her?"

"In a way," Sarah replied, "but it didn't help as much as I thought it would, and I don't want to do it again."

"Okay, I get that," Kate said, after a moment pondering.

"Do you?"

"Well, as much as I can. I mean, she was your friend and she basically stole your man from under your nose, but at the same time, she didn't kill him. That part was a total, tragic accident, so it leaves you angry at her, even when the very worst part of this whole thing isn't actually her fault."

Sarah stayed silent for a moment, soaking in her aunt's summary of events.

"Hearing that weirdly helps a bit, thank you."

"Look, one evening in an Irish pub isn't gonna solve everything," Kate replied, pretending to be more dismissive than she really felt. "I'm not gonna be so condescending as to say you'll get over it, or some crap, but I think you know it'll take time. Just let yourself have that time, and know that we're here for you along the way."

Kieran came back with a round of drinks, one cider, a small bottle of white wine, and a rosé spritzer. For Sarah, things started to feel a little better.

The evening went well in the busy but relaxed Irish pub, and Sarah's nap held off the effects of any jet-lag. Instead, she felt surprisingly rested, and relieved, for the first time in weeks. Maybe it was the vacation mode settling in, or maybe it was because she forgot how well she got on with her aunt and uncle. Whatever it was, it was a good start to her trip to Dublin.

Sarah insisted on buying the next round of drinks, despite Kate's polite protests, and warning of how expensive Ireland can be. She went up to the bar, and ordered the same again.

"That doesn't sound like a local accent at all," the barman noted, after he started to pour Kieran's pint.

"I'm Canadian," Sarah replied politely.

"Well, I hardly thought you were from Belfast, in fairness," he quipped with a cheeky smile on his face. "You here on holiday?"

"Yeah, I'm visiting family."

"Ah, that's good. Means you don't have to pay through the nose for accommodation! Welcome to Dalkey. Enjoy the Guinness, soak in the sea, and leave your worries far from these shores!"

Sarah giggled a little. "That sounds almost poetic, kudos."

"There's a bit of poetry in every town in this country, you just have to listen hard enough to enjoy it. Fifteen."

"Fifteen?"

"Fifteen euro? For the drinks?"

Sarah's cheeks reddened as the penny dropped, and she fumbled to take out the European cash from her purse.

"Didn't think I was that much of a smooth talker to distract you," the barman added, smiling as he took her cash.

"Don't get too cocky, I'm just not used to the accent just yet."

"Sure, because we're so terrible to listen to."

"I never said that, but I'll come back if I want to hear more poetry!"

"See that you do, Little Miss Canada."

Sarah smiled in spite of herself, as she gathered the three glasses in her hands and returned to her aunt and uncle, who were keeping an eye on the bar.

"I see you got chatting to Seán, anyway," said Kieran, as he picked up his pint glass.

"The barman? I didn't even get his name."

"I'd expect you to at least ask for that before flirting with a guy…"

"Kieran! I was merely being polite, he was the one practically reciting literature while I waited for the drinks. He was working for his tip, that's for sure."

"Yeah, there's only one thing about that," Kate added with a playful smile.

Sarah looked puzzled now. "What?"

"The Irish don't tip bar staff, not for drinks, anyway."

"Really?"

"We do tip," Kieran interjected, "but not in the way you guys do. We'll tip a waiter in a restaurant, or we might tip a lounge boy for bringing drinks over to your table, but you don't generally tip if you order at the bar or anywhere else. So, Casanova was performing for something other than a few euro, I reckon."

"Well, I wouldn't be interested anyway," Sarah dismissed.

"I thought as much," Kieran replied, "but I feel sorry for him."

"Why's that?"

"Because he keeps looking over at you every few seconds."

Sarah wanted to turn around towards the bar immediately, but she didn't want to make her assessment of the situation too obvious. After a few seconds, she turned back around to face the bar.

Seán, as she learned, was busy serving customers, but maybe wasn't the worst of guys. Six foot and broad, with short brown hair, wearing a blue sports jersey with a yellow harp on the left side.

If he were American, he'd probably be a quarterback at some high school team, but instead, this young Irishman probably played rugby or some local sport. Sarah couldn't deny that he was handsome, or cute at the very least, but she didn't want to think about anyone like that right now.

And then, he looked over, and their eyes locked for a split second, before he looked away, smiling.

7

Sarah slept soundly after her couple of welcome drinks at the pub in Dalkey, and woke up gently to the sound of seagulls calling nearby.

Eventually, she dragged herself away from the comfy bed and towards the balcony window, where she gazed across over Dublin Bay. The sun was shining—a rare occasion, Kieran had proclaimed before— and if it were any warmer, Sarah could've been mistaken for thinking she was somewhere else, like how she imagined Croatia or Greece to be. Either way, Ireland had a certain charm, and she felt a little better than she had done for a long while.

After a refreshing shower and choosing her outfit for the day, she made her way down towards the kitchen, where Kate was busy cooking breakfast.

"Good morning hon," Kate said warmly. "You've a choice for today - full Irish breakfast, or something a little lighter, maybe?"

"Nah, let's go with the full Irish. When in Rome, and all that jazz."

Kate served out a plate full of hearty food; two pork sausages, a thick slice of black and white pudding, fried mushrooms, a fried egg, a hash brown, some baked beans, and a slice of brown toast. The tea was already brewing in the ceramic teapot, placed in the middle of the oak table, and an empty mug awaited Sarah.

Sarah looked around. The house's décor was different enough to most Canadian homes, but it was difficult to say exactly how. It felt cozy, like how you'd imagine your grandmother's home, but it was still modern. The kitchen window looked out onto a small garden, and it was clear to Sarah that the house's main selling point was its sea views, but the garden was still quaint, and full of flowers from Kate's years of careful gardening.

Maybe it was the few soft touches, like a fridge magnet of Toronto, or the two small Canadian and Irish flags hanging from a coffee mug on a shelf, but Kate and Kieran's home felt enough like a home for Sarah, too. She was so many miles away from her mother, her friends, and everything else she had escaped, and yet she didn't really feel like she was 'abroad', exactly. It felt good.

"Any plans for today?", Sarah asked.

"Well, Kieran is at work," Kate replied, "and I've a business meeting in the city after lunch, so I thought we could get the train downtown and enjoy the morning for a while! You'll need to occupy yourself for an hour or so, but I can meet you afterwards and maybe go shopping, if you'd like. Or would you like to do something a bit more cultural?"

"No, that's perfect," Sarah replied, already enjoying the hearty breakfast. "I have plenty of time to do the touristy stuff later."

The suburban train ran along the coast and into the city, and the two got off at Pearse Station. They walked through the Georgian Quarter of the capital, past the statue of Oscar Wilde and the back of the Irish parliament building.

When they got to St. Stephen's Green, Dublin's own Central Park, they wandered around as they caught up on each other's lives. Kate had almost been in Ireland as long as she had grown up in Canada, but home would always be both places, she explained.

Her work at the Canadian embassy meant that they knew what was going on back in Toronto, sometimes better than Sarah would, and she'd occasionally travel back for a conference or two, or just to see family. Being married to Kieran meant that she couldn't plan every vacation opportunity to Canada, but instead, they mixed it up between trips around Europe and North America every other year.

Life was good in Dublin for Sarah's aunt, it seemed, and Sarah found herself wondering why she never really wanted to visit until Alice had gotten her the tickets. Even then, it was mainly an excuse to escape Jake.

Jake. She had almost forgotten about him. He was proud of how his grandmother was from Belfast, Sarah remembered, so he probably would've loved to have come to Ireland. She felt guilty for a moment, to be able to walk around that park on such a beautiful day, while he would've wanted to be there. But he wasn't.

8

Kate left Sarah on South William Street, which was clearly a cultural and social hub in the centre of Dublin. It was brimming with restaurants, boutiques, cafés, the occasional bar and pub, and a couple of beauty salons.

Hipsters rode their vintage-style bicycles, while she noticed two handsome guys holding hands as they walked towards St. Stephen's Green. It reminded her of Toronto's Church and Wellesley district, yet it had a distinctly more European vibe to it. It was her kind of place, she thought.

After a bit of window shopping, and a little retail therapy buying some Irish interior design gifts for her family back home, she decided to stop at the Metro Café. She ordered a coffee as she found one of only two tables free outside the street corner coffeehouse.

She allowed herself to soak in what she felt that afternoon; peace, serenity, and maybe a little acceptance. Whether she felt acceptance for herself, for Jake's death, or something else, she couldn't really tell.

She wasn't the same Sarah she was when Jake was alive, or when she still considered herself friends with Chrissy, but she felt like a small part of her was beginning to recognise that. More importantly, she could feel something within her say that she didn't need to be that Sarah anymore, if she didn't want to be.

"I see you're settling into Dublin life pretty well," a familiar male voice said, bringing Sarah out of her reflection.

"Seán, Hi!" Sarah's surprise was clear at the sight of the barman from the pub in Dalkey.

"I don't remember introducing myself properly to you", he said, puzzled. "How did you know my name?"

"Oh!" Sarah blushed quickly. "Um, my uncle noticed us chatting at the bar, he mentioned your name."

"Ah, okay," Seán replied, as he took the only other outdoor table left at the Metro Café, which just happened to be beside Sarah's, causing Sarah to become a little flustered.

"Besides, I'm in Ireland... Isn't every other guy called Seán around here?"

"Well, maybe in comparison to Canada, but we've a few other Gaelic names we like to use too. I just got stuck with one of the more popular ones."

Sarah looked down at her phone in an awkward attempt to look nonchalant. Did I just insult him?, she asked herself, wanting to hide a little. Seán caught the waitress' attention as she passed by, ordered an Americano, and took out his own phone. After a moment, Sarah noticed his head turned to look in her direction, only to turn back quickly.

She let out a little sigh of relief, smiling to herself; he wasn't exactly being subtle, but he was clearly trying not to intrude either. She put her phone away, knowing it should give him the signal that she's not too closed off from some small talk. Impressed with her own judgment of body language, Seán reacted as she expected.

"How are you finding Ireland so far?"

"It's beautiful. The scenery is gorgeous, and the people are really friendly, too. It's nice to get away from home for a while, so it was good timing to visit my aunt and uncle here. I'd like to see more outside of Dublin, but we've nothing planned just yet."

"Check out Belfast and Galway if you can," said Seán, "if you have time, anyway. Belfast is pretty cool for history and the Titanic Quarter, and Galway is really well known for the music scene and seafood. We're a small island, but there's a good amount to see here."

"Any tips for Dublin?"

"Depends how adventurous you want to be, or if you prefer being a city girl and sticking to shopping districts."

"What makes you think I'm all about shopping?"

"You mean apart from the interiors stuff beside you, and the fact that you're on one of Dublin's more fashionable streets?"

"Seán, so are you."

Seán looked stunned for a moment, before bursting out laughing.

"Touché! Okay, I'll give you that one. Fine: My top tip would be to do a little hillwalking around either the northern or southern tips of Dublin Bay. Both are headlands of sorts, which give you awesome views of the city. Some say that on a clear day, you can see across the sea to Wales, but I've never seen that far. Still, it's pretty epic."

"I'll have to see who'll be up for showing me around," Sarah replied, "but it sounds like a good idea."

"I'd offer to show you myself, but I don't want to be intrusive, especially if you have a boyfriend or something. I don't even know your name, actually."

"It's Sarah," she replied, shifting her weight in her seat. "And I did have a boyfriend, but not anymore. That's kinda why I'm here."

"Oh, I'm sorry," Seán said softly. "Was the break-up hard?"

"Well, you could say that I guess," Sarah replied, with a heavy sigh. "He died after he got hit by a car, so we technically never got to break up. Death kinda does that for you, instead."

Seán was visibly in shock over Sarah's backstory, or possibly over how she delivered it instead. His mouth opened a little, but he was stunned.

"Sarah, I dunno what to say at all – I'm so sorry."

"Why? You didn't know him, or me until recently."

"It doesn't matter. A few seconds should always be enough to feel empathy for someone. That's how I try to live, anyway. I've no idea what you're going through, and I certainly didn't mean to upset you by mentioning a boyfriend. I'm very sorry."

Sarah looked at Seán. Properly. He wasn't the confident, charming young man working at the pub. Instead, she saw a softness she hardly ever saw in a man his age. She saw an openness in him; not in a vulnerable way, but something more welcoming. Something more unassuming. Something that signalled to her that he wasn't a threat, or just some other guy she had to hold a shield against, like so many women have to do with so many men. She saw a friend in someone she didn't even know.

"Thank you, Seán."

9

After they ordered their second coffee at the Metro Café, Sarah learned more about her new friend. Seán wasn't from Dalkey, but a nearby suburb, and the pub where he worked belonged to his uncle. His father died when he was five, and the two spoke about how it felt to still miss their fathers at different holidays, no matter how long it had been since they passed away.

All the while, the sky over Dublin was clear and blue, a light breeze tickled Sarah's cheek, and she enjoyed the atmosphere around the city's streets. She also allowed herself, for the first time in a very long while, to enjoy the company of someone new.

The two slowly became lost in flowing conversation, talking about everything from history to politics to travel, until Sarah's phone buzzed and vibrated on her table. A new message from Kate: "Finished my meeting. Ready to go home?"

Sarah hesitated. Then she realised she was hesitating, and asked herself why. Which made her fall into a cycle of hesitation.

"Eh... Sarah?"

"Sorry?"

"I asked what your favourite part of Rome was...?" Seán looked a little puzzled, if not concerned, over Sarah's moment of staring at her phone. It took her another moment before she fully snapped out of her trance.

"Right, sorry! Urm... Ostia was a little outside the city, but I liked it a lot. It was great to be at the beach so close to the city."

"You okay?" Seán replied, almost ignoring Sarah's response entirely.

"Yeah, sorry, it's my aunt. She's ready to go back home."

"Ah, okay. Well, I can walk you to the train station, if you'd like?"

Seán was preparing to put his leather jacket back on, having taken it off during his earlier crash course lesson for Sarah on Irish history.

Sarah paused, looked back at the phone, and entered her trance-like state for a moment longer. Her frozen state brought back Seán's facial expression of patient concern, like when a dog knows its owner is ill.

"Sarah?"

His call prompted her back to life, but more than just to give her attention to him. She decided, for that moment, to stop holding herself back.

"Tell you what - I'll skip the escort to the train station and let you stay here to relax, on one condition."

"Eh…sure, okay," Seán replied, as he slowly sat back down in his seat, smiling. "What is it?"

"How about you take me on that walk you mentioned? I'd like to get a better view over the bay, if you're feeling up for taking this 'city girl' out?"

"I'd—yeah, I'd really like that".

Seán smiled with a glow, Sarah thought. Not a proud smile, like some cocky guy from back home. Not the smile of some jock who was used to getting his way with girls. Seán's smile was one of him being flattered, or maybe humbled. He wasn't a shy guy, exactly, but simply unassuming. He wasn't sweet in the clichéd sense of the word, but there was an innocence about him. He wasn't what she'd expected to meet in Ireland, but then again, a few weeks ago, she wouldn't have known she'd even be in this country.

Sarah gave him her phone number — WhatsApp was great for texting between international numbers — and she made her way towards the St. Stephen's Green shopping mall.
Kate was already waiting for her at its entrance, and smiled when she saw her niece approaching.

"Wow, it looks like you had a wonderful time. Did you go to the makeup counter at Brown Thomas?"

"Considering I don't even know where that is, I can only say no. Why?"

"Because you're glowing! What have you been up to?"

"Oh! Well, I just went shopping at the Powerscourt Centre, and then grabbed a coffee at the Metro. Dublin is really... well, it's full of little surprises, I guess!"

Kate took a second to look at her niece before she answered.

"For as much as I love Canada, maybe you can see why I fell in love with Ireland a little too."

"Yeah, totally. Is it time to go home?"

Kate started walking in the direction of the train station, pointing her elbow towards

Sarah to prompt her to link arms with her as they strolled along the street.

92

"I think so. You can tell me everything I've missed on our way back. So... see anything in particular that you liked?"

"Funny you should ask that," replied Sarah, blushing a little.

10

A few days had passed since Sarah had arranged to go for a hillwalk along the coast, and, after visiting some tourist hotspots in Dublin, Sarah's thoughts were now focused on her outdoors date with Seán (*was it really a date?* she caught herself thinking).

She thought she'd have to borrow hillwalking gear from her aunt, but Kate explained that it was the kind of coastal walk that could be done in jeans and a light jumper.

Dress code assigned, Sarah applied a little make-up nervously. She didn't want to overdo it, when it was meant to be a casual walk to explore more of Ireland, and yet she wanted to look good. Not for Seán, or maybe not just for him, but for herself as well. She knew she needed to let herself enjoy her time away from home.

Outfit ready for both mild winds and light socialising, Sarah walked towards the coastal train station near Kate and Kieran's home, and headed south towards Bray.

The view of the Irish Sea hadn't yet lost its appeal as the train moved along the coast, and she wondered if she'd ever get tired of it during her stay in Ireland. The water reminded her of her trips to Toronto Island as a child, and even though Lake Ontario was just that, a lake, the waves of the sea connected her with home—or maybe it just made her feel more at home in Dublin. She was abroad, yes, but not somewhere that felt foreign. She felt like she was just in another part of home.

The train eventually stopped at Bray station, where Seán had been waiting for her. Similar to Kate's advice, Seán was dressed suitably for the occasion; a blue polo shirt, navy tracksuit bottoms and white trainers. If it were a proper date, Sarah thought, he'd look a little too 'college jock' for her expectations of first date attire, but here, the outfit made complete sense.

Plus, he looked handsome. *Damn, Irish boys can impress*, she thought.

"Afternoon, Miss Canada," Seán greeted warmly. "Ready to explore a little?"

"Ready when you are, Mister Ireland," Sarah replied, striking a balance between sass and affection.

As they began their walk, and once the small talk of her train journey and a brief history of Bray was explained, Seán asked a little about where she grew up, and what suburban Toronto life was like.

Sarah replied somewhat cautiously; not for fear of revealing too much about her life, but more because the one man she didn't want to talk about kept springing to mind. Jake had attended the same schools she went to, he hung out in the same coffeehouses and, once they got older, bars. They went to the same university, despite studying different subjects.

Her home and her past were now haunted by her ex—her late—boyfriend, and every sentence she uttered to Seán now needed to go through a kind of whitewash on the path between her brain and her mouth. If Seán noticed the verbal cleansing, he didn't show it.

The day was brisk but clear. The blue sky stretched out across the Irish coast, as the sea met the beaches and rocky cliffs that Sarah and Seán walked past or over.

The southbound walk wasn't too challenging for Sarah, so instead of focusing on her physical endurance, she was able to simply enjoy the scenery and the company.

Some minutes later, though, her phone buzzed. A message from someone she hadn't thought about in quite some time:

> *Hey. I heard from your mom that you were abroad, so not sure if this is gonna wake you or whatever, but I need to tell you before you hear it anywhere else. I'm pregnant, and pretty sure it's Jake's. I'm deciding to keep it. I won't message you again beyond this, unless you want to talk, but I hope you realise this isn't meant to upset you. I just felt you deserved to hear it from me, rather than anyone else. C x*

Sarah froze as she read the message, leading Seán to walk on a little further before he realised that he had left his walking buddy behind. She stared at the message for a couple of seconds, but it felt so much longer.

"Hey, everything okay?" Seán asked.

Sarah couldn't move. Couldn't talk. She didn't hate Chrissy for messaging her, or even for her news. She was almost jealous for not being pregnant, although not fully—that would've been another weight on her grief. And yet, Chrissy now had within her a living remnant of Jake, and that realisation brought an inexplicable mix of joy, pity, warmth, and pain.

Séan slowly approached her, careful not to seem like he wanted to look at what she had read. Sarah looked up at him, tears welling in her eyes, feeling like a lost little girl.

"He could've been a father."

The tears took over and began to fall, prompting Seán to quickly throw his arms around Sarah. She let go, not unlike when her mother's shoulder became damp with tears outside the hospital, where Jake's family said goodbye to him.

Other walkers on the dirt trail by the coast walked by, some noticing Sarah sob into her Irishman's chest. One elderly lady asked softly if she was okay, but Sarah didn't look up, and Seán nodded with a polite smile.

"She's grand, yeah," he replied softly. "She just got a bit of bad news. Thanks."

"You'll be alright, pet," the old lady said. "You're loved, just remember that." She patted Sarah's back softly, making her look up at the kind-hearted lady. She reminded Sarah of her own grandmother, with blue eyes as gentle as Lake Ontario, and she smiled through her tears at her in gratitude.

11

Sarah and Seán walked on towards the next town on the coastal route, while Sarah opened up to her new Irish friend about the parts of the story she left out when she first mentioned Jake's death to Seán. It was a relief to tell someone who knew neither Jake nor her family, she felt, because Seán had no emotional baggage to cloud his judgment of the situation.

By the time they reached Greystones, Sarah was tired from the walk and the storytelling, so Seán suggested that they grab a coffee to relax.

At the café, Sarah took a seat after Seán offered to buy her coffee, joking that he wouldn't be surprised if she wanted some whiskey added to it.

While he ordered their drinks at the counter, Sarah took her phone out from her jacket pocket to look at Chrissy's message again. She examined every sentence, every word, every letter. She felt lighter after telling Seán what had happened, but the price of letting him in on the story was that Sarah could no longer escape it, despite being in Ireland. Regardless of her efforts, reality had been let back into her world, and it had clearly continued without her, miles across the seas.

When Seán returned with their coffees, Sarah didn't even look up.

"She'll actually be a really cool mom."

"Who? Chrissy?"

"Yeah. She used to babysit these kids who lived around the corner from my grandmother's house. She'd sing with the little girl on her karaoke machine, and when the older guy started dating a girl in school, she made sure to give him advice on how not to be a jerk. She never treated them as children, not really... just like people."

"Sounds like an aunt of mine, actually", Seán replied. "She's mad as a hatter. Gave me a glass of wine when I was thirteen and in some pub after a funeral. Dad went ballistic at her, but she was a legend in my eyes after that."

Sarah didn't reply to Seán's story. Instead, she continued to stare at her phone, lost in time, until Seán snatched it from her hand.

"Hey! What the hell!?"

"What next?"

"Excuse me?" Sarah wasn't impressed by her thieving coffee-buddy, who wore a disarming smirk in spite of her protests.

"What. Next. Right now, you're in Ireland, literally thousands of miles away from Chrissy, Jake, your friends, your family... practically speaking, what do you do next?"

Sarah stopped herself from reaching across the table, knocking over the coffee cups, and scrambling to take her phone back from Seán. She stared at him intensely, as if she was concentrating on moving him with her mind. Instead, she decided to accept his challenge.

"Move on... is that what you want me to say?"

"Not really", Seán replied, somewhat nonchalantly, "but let's take that as a start. How?"

"What do you mean 'how?'"

"How do you move on? How does anyone move on from the ordeal you've been through lately?"

Seán's tone changed in that reply, from calm and cheeky to passionately sympathetic, which threw Sarah completely. Here was a guy who had no reason to listen to some random girl on vacation in his neighbourhood. If his intentions were to get her into bed for some light holiday fun, talking about her dead ex-boyfriend wasn't going to get him hot and bothered. Well, hopefully not.

Sarah took a breath, and exhaled as she sat back in her seat, all the while maintaining eye contact with Seán.

"I don't know."

"That's bull. You *do* know. The only thing stopping you from realising that is that you're seeing it as one big, single unit of a mess. Instead, it's actually a mess made up of smaller messes."

Sarah's right eyebrow lifted itself towards the sky.

"Now you've lost me, dude."

Seán, exasperated at her reaction, grabbed a bunch of sugar packets from the ceramic bowl on the café table, and placed them in a pile between them.

"This is the mess as a whole, so let's look at it one by one. Chrissy's unborn child, for example."

Seán moved a sugar packet away from the pile and towards Sarah.

"Are you angry at it?"

"No! No... I mean, I once dreamt that *I'd* be the mother of Jake's child, but I can't hate a baby, especially one that isn't born."

"Good answer", Seán replied, moving the sugar packet away from Sarah and back into the bowl. "Next one: Chrissy. Do you hate the fact that she's pregnant with his child, and you're not?"

"Wow, don't hold back, Seán."

"Hey, it's not my dead boyfriend we're talking about, but it sure as hell beats staring at a phone."

Sarah took a breath as she looked at the second sugar packet.

"No. Not if he didn't love me. Not when I don't want kids just yet. Not now."

With that, Seán moved on to a third packet.

"Do you think you were responsible for them getting together?"

"No way, they made their own bed..."

Seán noted the vulnerable change in Sarah's voice, paused, and then placed the rest of the sugar packets back in their bowl. He took a long, slow sip of his coffee, not once taking his eyes off Sarah's face. When he placed his cup back down, her eyes lifted their focus from the sugar-free table, and met his own.

"I think," he said, "the rest of the questions you can answer yourself. One at a time, and in your own time, too."

The rest of their afternoon wasn't as filled with heavy conversation. Instead, the pair picked up the discussion about Rome that got interrupted by Kate in the city. They spoke about Seán's love for architecture, and how he travelled to Reykjavík to see his favourite architect's design for the Icelandic opera house.

Sarah found herself intrigued, lost, and entertained, all at the same time, as Seán tried to explain how Irish politics worked. Sarah described her various family trips around Canada; from the stunningly beautiful British Columbian scenery to the wild coastlines of Nova Scotia, coastlines not unlike those around Ireland.

Sarah found some familiarity in Seán too, and it deepened with every topic of conversation.

12

Sarah was reluctant to leave Greystones, where Seán had shown her so much more than just some scenery. She took the northbound train back with him towards Kate and Kieran's house in Dalkey, but Seán bid her goodbye as he got off a couple of stations before her destination. When she was alone, she took out her phone, and texted Kate to let her know she was on the way home. Then, she looked back at Chrissy's message, and decided to draft one of her own:

> *Thanks for letting me know. Congratulations. I'm in Ireland with family, not sure when I'm back. Take care.*

Sarah stared at what she wrote. It was polite, but cold. Then again, if she had expected to write any kind of message to her former best friend, she imagined that it would've included a lot more cursing. Seán was right, though, in spite of the weird sugar-packet symbolism, Sarah didn't hate the fact that Chrissy was pregnant. She just didn't know how else to let go of the pain and anger.

The following day, Kate and Kieran decided to take a few days off work to go on a road trip, to show Sarah around the north of Ireland. Sarah's great-grandmother was from Derry in Northern Ireland, so Kate had planned the trip to visit Belfast first for a night, then drive on towards Derry and stay with cousins, before driving back to Dublin. It was just what Sarah needed, but Kate seemed just as happy to relax, revelling in her ability to turn on her out-of-office mode for her work email.

Halfway through the two-and-a-half hour car journey from Dublin to Belfast, Sarah's phone vibrated - a WhatsApp message from Seán:

> *Really enjoyed the walk with you yesterday. Hope I wasn't too harsh at the café! Not sure what your schedule is like for the rest of your time here, but if you wanna hang out again before you leave for Canada, give me a shout. x*

"How's Seán?"

Sarah looked up towards the car's windscreen, where she noticed her uncle's eyes glancing between her and the road ahead.

"What makes you think it's from Seán," Sarah protested. "Actually, what makes you think it was a text?"

Kieran laughed heartily.

"Well, for one thing, two questions in quick succession is a *little* defensive. Besides, it's still the middle of the night in Canada-land, so I doubt it's your mother."

"Don't fall for an Irishman, Sarah," Kate warned with a smirk on her face. "They're more trouble than their charm leads you to believe!"

"Y'mean, the same charm that made you fall madly in love with me?" Kieran chuckled, and Sarah had to giggle at their flirtatious joking. They loved each other so much, and they never hid that. It was so cute to see.

"So, are you gonna see him again?" Kate asked, taking her gaze from her husband back to Sarah.

"Seán?"

"Well, unless you've met another cute Irish guy since you got here!"

"Oh! Is he *cute* now?" Kieran protested dramatically, pretending to be jealous.

"Come on, he is cute! What's wrong with that?!"

"You're selling him short," Kieran replied. "I'd say he's *gorgeous*, personally." The girls giggled at his metrosexual commentary.

"I dunno," Sarah dismissed. "He's a sweet guy, and it has been nice to hang out a little, but I dunno about seeing him again."

"Why not?," asked Kate.

"Y'mean, apart from my last boyfriend being dead?"

An awkward silence fell upon the car for a moment, which was strong enough to make Kate look back at the road ahead, and take a deep breath before turning back to her niece.

"Sarah, I didn't mean to be so disrespectful of your mourning for Jake, I'm sorry. I'm just happy to see that Seán was–"

"That he was what," Sarah interrupted. "Distracting me?"

"No, dear; that he gave you hope for a happier future."

It was some time before normality resumed between the three travelers, just before they made it into Belfast. When they checked into their hotel in the city, Kate gave Sarah a warm hug to show that she was sorry for upsetting her niece. Sarah responded in kind, knowing that there was no malice in her aunt's suggestions.

Kieran gave another hug to Sarah before leaving her to her own room, giving them all some time to refresh after the journey. Sarah decided to leave her clothes in her rucksack for another few minutes while she collapsed onto the bed, happy to have some time to herself.

She realized, in that moment, that maybe a family vacation wasn't the best way to heal after a dead, cheating boyfriend. While it sometimes took her mind off what had happened, it was also draining to be with family members who didn't want you to feel sad. They meant well, and she knew they wanted to make the most of her time in Ireland, but she just wanted to shut down and let go.

She did. She turned onto her side on the double bed, and cried as much as she had wanted to at the funeral. She cried as much as she would have, if Jake had been loyal. If Chrissy hadn't told her the truth by accident. If she had still been his love, her grief might have been so much easier to handle, but alone in that hotel room, her tears finally lost their bitterness, and flowed as they should have.

13

Sarah had drifted off to sleep after her emotional release, only to be woken up by a knock on her hotel room door. When she opened it, her uncle stood in the hallway, having already changed his outfit since the drive from Dublin.

"Hey – oh I'm sorry, did I wake you?"

"Don't worry about it," Sarah replied, rubbing the sleep from her eyes. "I hadn't planned to doze off, I guess the trip took it out of me more than I thought."

"Well, I was just letting you know that Kate is getting ready now, so we should be ready in about 20 minutes – or do you need more time?"

"No, that's cool. I'll get ready now."

"Okay." Kieran took a step back to leave her to it, when he stopped himself. "We love you, Sarah."

"Thanks, Kieran, I love you guys too," she replied, caught off-guard. "Where did that come from?"

"Just the little moment in the car. I don't want you to think that we're not here for you."

"Hey, that's pretty obvious, trust me. You guys have done so much for me since I got here. Thank you."

Kieran blushed a little, gave a nod of appreciation for his niece's words, and walked towards the elevator, leaving Sarah to close her room door, smiling.

She took out her phone, and opened WhatsApp to realise that she hadn't replied to Seán's earlier message. She read over it again, smiled, and started to tap away on her screen:

> *Hey, sorry for the delay. We just arrived in Belfast for a night. Going to Derry tomorrow for another night, but coming back to Dublin after that. And no, you weren't harsh at all, it might have been just what I needed. Might not look at sugar the same way again, though. ;-) Hanging out again sounds like a great idea, let me know what you have in mind. S x*

Sarah could feel a small part of herself speak from a hidden part of her mind as she pressed *Send* on her phone's screen: *Just go with it, and enjoy it while you're here.*

Belfast was a surprisingly enchanting city, which Sarah hadn't expected. The three of them had dinner in a gorgeous Parisian-styled restaurant overlooking the city hall, before going to a modern Irish bar in the northern Cathedral Quarter of the city, surrounded by other pubs and restaurants.

There was a buzz of energy to Belfast that felt different to Dublin, but she thought there was more of a British look to the place, also.

They jumped into one of the iconic black taxi cabs that reminded her of television shows set in London, and the driver gave them a tour of the murals of the Falls Road, the Shankill, and Titanic Quarter districts. Belfast was steeped in history, and Sarah was smitten from the very start.

The following day, Kate decided to drive instead of Kieran, which suited him perfectly as he felt a little hungover from the beers that finished off the night at the hotel bar.

The drive to Derry was just as scenic as the journey from Dublin, and Sarah allowed herself to enjoy the trip a little more than she did before.

Once they arrived at their cousins' house, a roast dinner was presented, before exploring the city's famous walls, and the stylish Peace Bridge that crossed the River Foyle.

Derry definitely felt more like a big town to Sarah, but it was just as charming and interesting as anywhere else she had discovered on the Emerald Isle.

The following morning, it was time to say goodbye to the cousins she had just met, thanking them for their hospitality, and for showing them around their city.

Kieran drove back to Dublin, taking just over three hours, while Kate and Sarah chatted about everything they had seen, family history, and the history of Northern Ireland's Troubles. When they got back to Dalkey, the sun was shining, and it felt like coming home.

Once Sarah's phone reconnected to WiFi, she saw a Skype message from her mother:

> *Hi honey, hope you're enjoying yourself! Give me a call when you get a moment. Love you xx*

Sarah noticed that her mom's status was *Online now*, so she didn't waste any time. The call took a second to connect, and soon she heard her mother's sweet, warm voice.

"Well hello! How's my wandering girl?"

"Hey Mom! We're just back from seeing Siobhán and Thomas in Derry, they put us up for the night, and we went out in the city after dinner. We were in Belfast the night before, too. How are you?"

"Oh honey, that's wonderful news! Gosh, I think it has been twenty years since I've seen them at your uncle's wedding in Dublin."

"Yeah," Sarah replied, "they mentioned that. How are things there?"

"Yes... they're fine."

"Mom? What's up?"

Sarah could hear her mother take a breath before she responded.

"Well, I don't really want to go into it on the phone much, and it can wait until you're back..."

"Mom, spit it out."

Another intake of breath.

"Well, I went to the doctor on my lunch break a few weeks ago, and I didn't want to say anything at the time, because I wasn't sure if I was being paranoid. It turns out that they've found a lump."

This cannot be happening, Sarah thought to herself, *not again. Not now.*

"Where?"

"My breast. They don't know yet if it's benign, but I imagine it is, and it'll be a quick operation. I'll be fine, it's just been on my mind, that's all."

"Okay," Sarah replied, now sure of herself. "I'll come back right away."

"Don't you dare!" Her mother now sounded like Sarah had just insulted her. "There is no point at all in coming home when I feel perfectly fine, and it would end up being a small procedure. *Promise me*, Sarah."

Sarah paused. She didn't like the idea of staying when her mother possibly had cancer, but she was still right. Coming home and adding to the worry was pointless, when neither of them knew any more.

"On one condition: If you need to go for a biopsy or anything, keep me updated. I don't like you going through this on your own."

"Okay, promise," her mother softly confirmed. "Now, tell me everything about your trip so far. What do you think of Dublin?"

Sarah proceeded to tell her everything, from exploring the country to meeting Seán, all the while thinking that her mother now needed a distraction just as much as Sarah once did.

14

Sarah held her mug of Earl Grey tea firmly, taking comfort from its warmth, as she told Kate about her mother's news. A tense, concerned silence fell upon the sitting room, while Kieran prepared turkey for dinner. Kate was equally concerned for her sister as Sarah was for her mother, knowing that neither of them could just click their heels together and return to Toronto.

"Did she say anything about the lump," Kate asked, looking into the stove's animation of flames.

"Just that she discovered it and went for a check-up. I guess they have to do a mammogram first, before they decide if a biopsy is needed."

Kate nodded in silence, not really knowing whether to be vocal in how worried she was, or to restrain herself so her niece wouldn't feel worse than she did herself. She eventually chose the latter, for Sarah's sake.

"Even if it is benign, it's good that she - we - know now. If not, then they'll be able to remove it simply enough, I reckon."

"You sure?"

There was something in Sarah's voice that was different to before, even unlike when she had spoken about Jake. Jake's death was a mixture of heartache and grief, but this was a vulnerable feeling of helplessness that Kate recognised more, because she saw it in Alice when Sarah's father died. She got up from the armchair and sat beside her niece to give her a cuddle, something they both needed in that moment.

"I'm sure of it, kiddo. Your mom will be fine, and so will you. Next time you visit, she'll have to come over as well, and we'll be in Canada for Christmas too. It'll all be fine by then, trust me".

***

The following morning, Sarah woke up to find a text message from Seán waiting for her:

> *Hey! How was the trip back from Derry? I was wondering if you'd be up for dinner in the city later tonight? My treat. Seán x*

Sarah noticed the *x* in the message, and smiled. Maybe she blushed - it had been so long since she had that sensation - but either way, waking up to read his text was nice.

She wrote back and agreed to his suggestion, now accepting that she wanted to see him again. After she got up, showered, and went down to the kitchen for breakfast with Kate and Kieran, Sarah asked if Kate could drop her to a shopping mall on her way to work.

"Of course, honey," Kate replied warmly, "but what for?"

"I want to give myself a day of retail therapy," Sarah replied, "but I might also have a date later."

Kate almost dropped her glass of orange juice in a mixture of excitement and disbelief.

"Well, that was one answer I was *not* expecting at this hour of the morning! No prizes for guessing who the lucky guy is!"

"I don't know what you mean!" Sarah seemed to glow as she finished her cup of coffee.

"Uh-huh, sure, honey," her aunt teased. "Anyway, you absolutely shall go to the ball, my princess. Take this as well, for the taxi back here after your shopping spree, and keep the change for your night out." Kate produced one hundred euro from her purse, and passed it towards Sarah on the marble countertop. Sarah was surprised at how much money she was being offered.

"How much will the taxi be?"

"Around twenty, I reckon."

"Eighty euro change? Are you sure?"

Without answering, Kate walked around to Sarah's side of the countertop to give her niece a cuddle and a kiss on the forehead.

"You deserve a good night out, sweetheart. Make it count."

Sarah got out of the car at a shopping mall that Kate recommended, the Dundrum Shopping Village. She wandered around some of the clothing stores until she found a red velvet dress, and fell in love with it instantly. When she tried it on, it looked like it was made for her figure, and she almost ran to the checkout. She couldn't wait to tear off the price tag and wear it, and show it off to herself in the mirror. She also couldn't wait for Seán to see it.

When he did, later that evening in the city, he was visibly and audibly stunned, with a "Wow!" that slipped from his lips as she walked up to him outside the Italian restaurant he suggested.

"I take it that's a good reaction," Sarah teased.

"I think you're even more deserving of the title I originally gave you - Miss Canada."

"Thanks, but I'm glad I'm not a pageant queen. I like my food too much."

"I knew there was a reason I liked you."

As Sarah blushed at her date's understated flirting, Seán turned to face the restaurant's entrance, and opened the door for her. He had reserved a table for them both by the window, where they could take part in people watching as they waited for their various courses. He pulled out Sarah's chair for her, insisted that she chose wine for the table, and made sure that she ordered first.

Once the waiter walked off with their order, Sarah took a moment to appreciate the effort Seán put into his own clothes for their dinner date.

He wore brown leather shoes, beige chinos, a white shirt with the top two buttons open, showing just a little of his broad chest, and a navy blazer. Sarah couldn't deny that he looked gorgeous, and almost effortlessly so. Even more, the effort he put into his outfit made hers all the more worthwhile, and she enjoyed that little moment of appreciation all the more.

The conversation flowed easily between them throughout dinner. Sarah recalled her family trip to Ulster with Kate and Kieran, and Seán wanted all the details, from what she thought of Belfast to her time in Derry. By the time it came to dessert, Seán suggested a game of rapid-fire twenty questions.

"This could get messy," Sarah joked.

"Only if you think about it too long," he replied.

"Go: Colour."

"Red. You?"

"Purple. Sport?"

"Ice hockey."

"Obvious choice for a Canadian," Seán quipped.

"Touché! Okay, you?"

"Rugby. *Duh*."

"Fair. Ideal vacation spot?"

"Oslo," replied Seán. "It was beautiful. You?"

"San Francisco. There was this little place you could get the world's best Irish coffee. Amazing."

"I'll have to try to make you an Irish coffee, in that case, and see which one you prefer."

"You'd have some stiff competition," warned Sarah, "these guys are world renowned!"

"And I'm not?"

"Well, I never heard of you until I got here!"

"Hopefully you'll think of me when you go back!"

Sarah blushed instantly. Seán smiled, satisfied. The waiter arrived just in time with their ice-cream.

For the whole night, Seán had a glint in his eye, and Sarah had never been happier. That was before he took her to a quiet pub, ordered a night cap, and kissed her tenderly.

Even then, she couldn't stop smiling.

15

That night, Sarah dreamt that she was running along the coast as the sun set across Dublin Bay. Then, she leapt into the air, and started to float. She leaned forward, and started moving like a dolphin would in the sea as it swam. With each fluid movement, she started to fly, stronger and faster, happy with her newfound powers of flight and freedom.

When she awoke, soft sunshine flooded the guest bedroom, which now felt like her room in Kate and Kieran's house.

She realised that she slept soundly and comfortably for the first time in weeks, if not months. Once she eventually accepted that she wouldn't drift back to her dolphin-like flight dream, she rubbed the sleep out of her eyes, and turned over to her bedside table to pick up her phone.

A message had been waiting for her to wake up:

> *"Good morning, gorgeous. Hope you got home okay. Had an amazing night with you. S xx"*

Sarah beamed with a smile, lying back on her pillow and reminiscing about last night's date. Seán had been the perfect gentleman, but with a humour and energy that she had never expected from guys back home. He had a playful charm, a desire to connect and make the most of the night, and to feel lighter. Sarah had to admit to herself, finally, that she was starting to fall for him.

Resigning herself to the fact that she had to get up eventually, Sarah got out of bed and went about her morning routine, even though it was closer to midday than morning. When she got down to the kitchen,

Kate was sitting at the dinner table with a cup of coffee, and a half-full cafétiere beside it.

"Good morning, princess," her aunt greeted warmly. "Good night?"

"I can't even deny it," Sarah replied, "it was simply amazing".

"I'm glad to hear it," Kate said. "You truly deserve it. Coffee?"

Sarah nodded as she walked over to the table and pulled out a chair opposite Kate's. Kate had the day off work to look after a few things for the charity she volunteered with, but she still dressed like she was going to the office.

"Sarah, I got a call last night while you were out." Kate's voice sounded somber enough to stop Sarah from lifting the cafetiere off the table, giving her aunt her full attention.

"Your mom collapsed at work yesterday. She was brought to hospital, and she regained consciousness pretty quickly, but the doctors have pushed forward the biopsy to tomorrow, because they fear it might be related. When I spoke to the doctor on the phone, they had just taken some blood tests, so I don't know what the results of those were yet. I'm thinking it might be a good idea to go back home, the two of us."

Sarah's heart beat hard in her chest, but she nodded quickly before feeling her eyes begin to water. That prompted Kate to jump up off her seat and run around the table to cuddle her niece, knowing the panic and worry that was taking hold on them both.

"Shhh, I know honey, I know. I'll book the flights today and we'll try to go tomorrow. We both need to go home."

Knowing that it would be a few hours until daybreak in Toronto, Sarah went upstairs to pack everything she could, with the exception of a different outfit for the following day, into her luggage.

Kate did as she promised, and booked a morning flight directly from Dublin for the next day, while Kieran said that he'd be ready to come over if Kate needed him to.

Within an hour, the bedroom Sarah had come to love and see as her own had returned to feeling like a guest room, with her own presence now back in her bags.

She took out her phone and texted Seán back, asking to meet her if he was free. He offered to take her for coffee near her house, so she could easily get back if Kate heard from the hospital back home.

When Seán drove to the house, Sarah ran out and wrapped her arms around him, not even giving him time to close the car door after he got out.

"I feel so helpless, I wish I could do something."

"I know," Seán said, "I wish I could do more than offer a cuddle and a cappuccino."

Sarah smiled softly, in spite of herself. "Don't worry, it's probably exactly what I need right now. Thank you."

"For what?"

"For being here," Sarah replied, "for trying to look after me. For *wanting* to."

"You deserve it and a lot more, trust me. You're the most genuine girl I know. I'm gonna miss you so much, but I wouldn't want you to stay here a minute longer, considering the circumstances."

Sarah straightened up at what Seán had just said.

"I hadn't even thought of that."

"Which?"

"That I'm leaving you behind here. God, it didn't even occur to me."

Seán smiled at her, and tilted his head slightly. "Sarah, I'm not upset that you're thinking about your mother more than me right now. At least I got a sneaky kiss in last night."

Sarah's face softened slightly at his compliment, before returning to her state of worry.

"I know, it's just that meeting you was just what I needed here, but I don't want to forget you just because I have to go."

"You do realise that it's the 21st Century, and WhatsApp and the rest of the world's social apps work around the planet? Well, most parts of the planet, anyway."

"Yeah, I know but -"

"But nothing," Seán said, cutting across her. "We both know I'd love to see you again, and maybe we can arrange that at some point, but right now, that's not important. I'm here for you now, today. When you leave tomorrow, you'll look after your mother if and when she needs you. And she'll always need you, she's your mammy."

Seán reached his hand across to hold Sarah's, before picking it up to kiss it across the table.

"I'm only a text away. I promise."

16

After another long flight, Kate and Sarah eventually got through to the arrivals hall of Toronto Pearson International Airport, and made their way to where their Uber driver would meet them. They were jet-lagged from the flight from Ireland, but they both agreed that they wanted to see Alice as soon as possible, so resting at home could wait a little longer. The ride to City Hospital provided a little opportunity to nap, but neither of the women felt comfortable enough to be able to try.

When the car arrived outside the hospital, Sarah got flashbacks of the last time she was there, holding Jake's sister's hand as she was led to his bereaved parents. For as concerned as Sarah was for her mother, at least she knew she was alive. She knew she'd be able to give her a hug that day, even if there would be tougher times ahead.

What she didn't know, however, was that by the time she and Kate would reach Alice's hospital room, a familiar face would be right beside her, holding her mother's medical chart.

"The doctor will be around tomorrow, and until then, I can prescribe some…"

The nurse's words trailed off as she noticed her old friend enter the room.

"Sarah, hi."

"Chrissy, hey."

"I didn't know you were back home."

"We only landed, like ninety minutes ago, max."

"Chrissy," Alice interrupted, "can you give us a few moments? They're just off the plane."

"Wow, yes of course. I'll let you guys catch up." Chrissy was visibly thrown by Sarah's appearance, despite knowing that with Alice in hospital, seeing her was a strong possibility. "Welcome back, by the way."

Chrissy placed Alice's chart back in its holder at the bottom of her bed, and walked out of her room. Sarah noticed her bump, but said nothing more, as she watched her sheepishly make her exit, and focused more on being able to spend time with her mother.

"You two look like you need a nap," Alice remarked with a soft, relieved smile on her face.

"I'd rather a vodka, to be quite honest," Kate half-joked.

"You're too early, the cocktail trolley doesn't come around until after dessert. I can imagine a shot of whiskey is handed out in Irish hospitals, though."

"Only if there's no penicillin left, maybe."

"Much as I love the jokes," Sarah interjected, "we didn't cross the Atlantic for a comedy show." She looked at her mother in a half-stern, half-worried-to-death look, and reached over to hug her in her hospital bed.

"I know, honey, I'm not the best comedian, either. Thank you for coming."

"What's the latest?"

Alice sighed.

"They don't know what made me collapse, but they did the biopsy yesterday, and did blood tests, too. The results aren't due back for a few days, so they're keeping me in until tomorrow. The consultant seems relatively upbeat about the whole thing, though, especially if the biopsy brings good news."

"But that doesn't explain the fainting," Kate added, making Alice shrug her shoulders.

"No, but that could be anything from stress at work to the menopause. At least if we rule out cancer, then we can deal with the rest more easily."

Sarah didn't like hearing the word *cancer* at all, but to her own surprise, and despite the ordeal of long-distance travel, she felt quite practical, if not optimistic.

"You're right, Mom. Plus, you probably have the best medics in the city by your side."

"Probably," Alice chuckled lightly. "Actually, there are a few young doctors here that are *very* easy on the eye, Sarah. Once you're ready to get back out there, I mean."

"Mom!" Sarah's cheeks reddened, but her smile belied her supposed shock.

"Well if you won't have them..."

"Alice!"

The laughter echoed throughout the hospital ward's corridor - a sound that wasn't often heard around there.

17

The following morning, Sarah woke up in her own bed for what felt like the first time in ages. Unlike the last time, though, she no longer felt numb or broken. A weight had been lifted from her shoulders since seeing her mother, and although they'd still have to wait for the biopsy's results, hopes and spirits were raised simply by the three women being together.

Sarah picked up her phone, and saw that Seán had sent a message while it was the middle of the night for her Canadian home:

"Good morning beautiful! Hope you slept well. Thinking of you from across the ocean - let me know how your mam is getting on when you can. S xx"

She smiled to herself, comforted that Seán was still thinking of her, despite her having left Ireland. Sitting up in her bed, she wrote back:

"Hey handsome, good afternoon! ;-) Things are good here, although it's a bit weird to be back, in some way. Mom is doing well, waiting for test results. Miss you xxx"

She didn't appreciate until that point how much she would have missed Seán. He had been there for her, even though he didn't need to be.

When she got herself ready for the day, Kate was already down in the kitchen, preparing breakfast.

"Good morning, hon," Sarah's aunt said, with a lightness in her voice.

"Morning. How did you sleep?"

"Meh. The same kind of jet-lag that I'm used to whenever I come back home."

Sarah paused for a moment. "Is it still home?"

"Here?"

"Yeah - Toronto. Canada."

Kate took a step back from the kitchen counter and stared out the window.

"Yes and no. It's where I grew up, it's where I know how everything works, like it's a part of my own body. I've spent a *lot* of time in Ireland, though, so that's home, too. Canada is my childhood home, but Dublin is the home of who I am today... if that makes sense."

"Yeah, it does," replied Sarah pensively. "Like, where you're from doesn't necessarily mean that's where you're meant to be, but you'll still be familiar with it."

"Exactly." Kate looked at Sarah with a soft smile. "How are you?"

"Fine, I slept well enough I -"

"I don't mean this morning," Kate clarified. "I mean in general. Jake. Your mom. Ireland. You. Seán."

Sarah already knew that Kate hadn't meant about her jet-lagged lack of sleep. She sighed, walking over to the breakfast bar in the kitchen to sit down.

"I dunno. When I feel good, or even mildly okay, I'm hit with this wave of self-awareness, and I become guilty, as if I shouldn't enjoy myself when Jake isn't dead that long. When I feel angry, a small voice in my head tells me that there's no point in wasting my life in some pointless rage. When I was with Seán, I could feel a hope inside myself again, but it was up against this feeling that I was cheating on Jake. Then there's Chrissy."

"Yeah, that was awkward in the hospital yesterday," Kate added.

"It was, but I know she's hurting, too. She's pregnant with Jake's child, but I don't hate her for what happened with Jake. I'm hurt that she betrayed me, that she thought she could get away with not telling me what happened."

"I get you," said Kate, "but if there's such a thing as karma, then it's got a cruel side: She is going to raise a child without its father being around. Even if Chrissy finds a partner to eventually step in as a father figure, it'll still be difficult. That kid won't ever know who its father was."

"Which is kind of why I can't feel angry anymore," Sarah replied. "Not for too long, at least."

Kate, seeing her niece maturing before her eyes, knew better than to continue with the wellbeing check-in.

"Come on, let's go in to see your mom."

Sarah and Kate were the first to hear the good news when they returned to the hospital. Alice had already had a visit by one of the oncologists that morning, who was able to confirm that the lump was benign, and although it didn't explain her fainting, she could be deemed healthy enough to be discharged.

Alice already looked healthier when her sister and daughter went to her room.

Sarah and Kate immediately helped to pack her things.

But just before they were about to leave, Sarah noticed a familiar figure walk past the doorway.

"Hey, guys, can you give me five minutes before we go?"

"Of course, honey," replied her mother, knowing already why Sarah wanted the time.

Sarah walked out to the corridor, where she noticed Chrissy standing against the nurses' station counter. She didn't notice Sarah approaching.

"Thank you."

"Ohmygosh," Chrissy blurted out, startled by Sarah's skills of stealth. "You scared the crap outta me!"

"Sorry. I just wanted to say thank you for looking after my mom while she's been here."

"Oh Sarah, of course," Chrissy replied, almost pleading. "Once I saw her name on the patients' list, I made a point of making sure she was okay. She's been like a second mom to be, and after everything, um, we've been through... well, it's my pleasure."

Sarah scanned her former friend, her demeanour, her words, and how she almost squirmed for Sarah's forgiveness. Chrissy never looked lost before, even when they were children. Chrissy was the confident one, and Sarah was the softer, quiet one. Now, the roles were almost reversed.

It made Sarah realise something else, as well. She had grown stronger in herself, without even noticing the change.

"Well, I just wanted to say that I'm grateful," Sarah confirmed, trying to sound sincere while still being somewhat guarded. "It means a lot, after everything we've been through."

Chrissy stopped squirming at the sound of her once-best friend repeating her last utterance, and smiled softly at Sarah.

"See you around, Chrissy."

Chrissy shyly waved at Sarah as she turned to rejoin her mom and aunt and head home. Sarah felt something within her that she hadn't experienced in a while, but it felt like only part of a change. The second part was waiting for her elsewhere in the city, and she asked Kate to drive her there after they dropped Alice back home.

18

The sky cleared to become a beautiful, bright blue, as Kate drove the pair towards the graveyard where Jake was buried, an unexpected destination at the request of her niece. When the roads were clear enough to take her eyes off them for a second, Kate would glance over at Sarah, and noticed a serenity that she had not seen in her before; not as a child, not on her occasional visits back to Canada with Kieran, and not as a grief-stricken young woman in Ireland. This was a state of being that Kate hadn't seen in Sarah before, but it was more relieving than alarming, and it didn't warrant breaking the silence in her car as she drove.

Once they reached the graveyard, Kate found a place to park her car, and turned off the engine before turning to her niece.

"I can stay in the car, if you'd like a moment."

"Would that be alright?"

"Of course! I understand. Take your time and come back whenever you're ready."

Sarah unfastened her seat belt and reached over to hug Kate warmly, kissing her on her cheek as she pulled away and opened the passenger door. After a minute or so of walking up towards Jake's plot, Sarah noticed a familiar solitary figure standing nearby, looking at Jake's headstone. She didn't hear Sarah approach until her name was added to the light breeze.

"Maggie?"

"Sarah!" Maggie stretched out her arms towards her and welcomed a hug.

"I heard from your mother you went abroad for a while, when did you get back?"

"A couple of days ago. I was visiting family in Ireland."

"Yes, your mom said something about Europe. It's so good to see you."

Maggie's eyes began to mist, before she broke her gaze away from Sarah to look towards Jake's headstone.

"It's hard to believe that it's been long enough for the soil to settle into place," Maggie said, more to herself than to her new companion. "Only yesterday, I was tidying his room, and I still felt anxious to finish the dusting in time, so I could have dinner ready for him when he'd..."

"Come back," Sarah added, joining in.

"Yes. He'd be so bad at telling me where he was going, or if he was visiting friends after college or work, that his dinners were almost always cooked a second time before he'd eat them. Except when you came to visit, of course; then, he'd want everything just right. He'd ask me what I planned to cook, or if he could help, or if he could cook something instead."

"I remember when he tried to melt chocolate to coat some strawberries," Sarah recalled, chuckling a little.

"Oh God! Yes! How that boy thought frying chocolate was a good idea... well, he definitely wasn't going to win any cooking awards, but his heart was always in the right place."

Maggie didn't seem ready to reminisce over her late son too much, Sarah noticed, as

Maggie started to weep silently, before stopping herself.

"Oh, actually, I have something for you."

Maggie opened up her leather handbag and rummaged around in it for a moment, before producing a white envelope, offering it to Sarah. Sarah instantly recognised how her name was written on it.

It was Jake's handwriting.

"This was in his jacket on the day he... well, on the day. I completely forgot about it, but I had intended to give it to you on the day of his funeral. Obviously, I just forgot, with everything else going on that day."

"Of course, I understand." Sarah reached out for the envelope, examining the handwriting.

After all this time, she thought. *All those messages and calls, trying to get through to him that day, and only now I'm seeing his last message. A letter.*

"I'll let you open it in private," Maggie said. "Hopefully it will be of some comfort."

"Do you know what it is?"

"I haven't a clue, honey," Maggie replied, her voice heavy with a blend of sorrow, sympathy, and curiosity for what her son's final letter said. "All I know is that if it was in his jacket, he was planning to give it to you that evening."

Maggie stepped forward to give Sarah a long, comforting hug, one they both needed. Sarah knew that it was the last time she would see Maggie or any of Jake's family for a long while, and that this was their final goodbye. Maggie kissed Sarah's forehead, released her from her embrace, and waved before turning to walk away.

Once Maggie was far enough away, Sarah opened the letter Jake had written for her:

Dear Sarah,

If you're reading this, it means that I didn't have the heart to do it in person, and that means that I have so much more to apologise about. I have no idea how to do this, and writing a letter is not the easiest way, but at least I can try to express myself. By now, you will probably hate me, but I need to be honest with you.

I let you down in so many ways, and I don't think I'm ready yet to be anyone's boyfriend right now. I want to travel the world, but I want to be single during that adventure. I want to meet people and have wild nights in random places that will happen only once, before I eventually have to face the expectations of my family, my friends, and the world. Find a woman to be my wife. Start a family. Settle down with the house, the kids, and the SUV for the typical country drives and weekends away.

Maybe I'll grow old enough to want that, but right now, it's not me. I've made some serious mistakes while I've been your boyfriend, and while I know I've hurt you in the process, it has proven to me that I really don't want to be in a serious or stable relationship. I want to be having crazy, unpredictable experiences that I know I should be having at my age, but not at your expense. It's not worth hurting you, but that's why I need to say goodbye now.

Sarah, you are such an amazing woman. I mean it when I say I care for you, regardless of what you think of me now. You deserve to find a man who wants to be with you, who is ready to love, and strong enough to commit, because I honestly think that does take strength of character. That's something I need to work on, but I'll hopefully learn in time.

Take care of yourself. Don't ever give up on love, because it's what you do best.

Love, always,
Jake

Sarah took a moment to let his words sink in, like a new tattoo slowly drying into freshly punctured skin. She could hear his voice in every word, yet for all the pain she felt as she read his letter, she couldn't tell if the pain was her own, his, or theirs combined.

Now, though, it made sense, she thought. Chrissy hadn't stolen Jake at all; he was going to break up with Sarah, and tell Chrissy that he wasn't interested in her, either.

He deserved to be happy, just like she did, but he didn't deserve to leave this world so soon. He was so young, and she realised the gravity of that with his letter. He was still trying to learn who he was and what he wanted, on a level that he never told her, because he couldn't express it.

Yet, in spite of his flaws, his mistakes, and the hearts he broke on the way, she still would have loved to have said goodbye, and that they'd both be okay.

Sarah realised in that moment that she could forgive Jake – not because she could justify what he did, but because he wasn't lucky enough to make any more young mistakes.

"Goodbye, Jake," she whispered to his grave, as lovingly as she once spoke to him long ago. She stepped over to the headstone and kissed it softly, before she turned to walk towards the graveyard's iron gates.

Epilogue

"How's he sleeping?"

"Better nowadays, although I can only imagine what he's going to be like when he starts teething!"

"I don't know how you're able to do it," Sarah replied, smiling down at the carrier.

"Neither do I, but I guess you just have to!"

Chrissy smiled as she looked at Sarah cooing over her sleeping baby boy at their feet, while she managed to enjoy her cappuccino. Little baby James definitely had his father's eyes, and Sarah took a bittersweet comfort in seeing them again.

He may not have expected to be a dad, and Sarah never thought that Chrissy would be the one to have his child, but the pain of that revelation faded in the last couple of months. Meeting James for the first time sped up the healing process, because Sarah felt that part of Jake now lived on in baby James.

"Are you going to come and visit?" Sarah asked.

"Sure! Once this little tiger gets old enough to fly, although I dunno how he'll manage on a seven-hour flight. Maybe next year."

"No pressure," Sarah replied, her eyes still fixated on James as he wriggled in his carrier. "I'll be back for Thanksgiving at least, so we can catch up then, if not sooner."

"Are you scared?"

"Of what?"

"Starting a new life so far from home."

"That's the thing, Chrissy," Sarah replied. "It already *is* home - just a different kind of home. It's where I want to be."

Chrissy beamed with a warm, peaceful smile.

"I am so happy for you, Sarah."

The two got up from their seats outside Dixie's Coffeehouse, where they had spent so many hours during their teenage years, and gave each other a warm, caring hug.

It had taken three months for their friendship to be rebuilt since Sarah's return to Canada, and even though they both knew it would never be the same, Sarah felt at peace with that.

Forgiveness was the last thing that her childhood home had taught her, the last lesson before she considered herself a real grown-up. Now, she was ready.

Later that day, Sarah hugged her tearful mother tightly in the Departures hall of Toronto Pearson International Airport. She checked in for her flight, and dropped off her luggage at the desk. She went through Security, and when she got a coffee at one of the many cafés by the terminal gates, she took a photo for her Snapchat and added the caption:

"Next stop: Dublin. So happy to start a new story."

Eight hours and an ocean crossing later, Sarah stepped through the Arrival gates of Dublin Airport, where Seán stood waiting for her, holding a single red rose.

"Welcome back, Miss Canada."

***